Jack and the Beanstalk

Jack be Nimble

Jack be nimble,
Jack be quick,
Jack jump over
The candlestick.

Jack and Jill

Jack and Jill went up the hill
To fetch a pail of water;
Jack fell down and broke his crown,
And Jill came tumbling after.

The House that Jack Built

This is the farmer sowing his corn
that kept the cock that crowed in the morn
that waked the priest all shaven and shorn
that married the man all tattered and torn
that kissed the maiden all forlorn
that milked the cow with the crumpled horn
that tossed the dog that worried the cat
that killed the rat that ate the malt
that lay in the house that Jack built.

Little Jack Horner

Little Jack Horner
Sat in the corner,
Eating a Christmas pie;
He put in his thumb,
And pulled out a plum,
And said, What a good boy am I!

First published 1993 by Walker Books Ltd
87 Vauxhall Walk, London SE11 5HJ

This edition produced for
The Book People Ltd, Hall Wood Avenue
Haydock, St Helens WA11 9UL

Printed in Hong Kong

ISBN 0-7445-2613-2

Come Back, Jack!

Catherine and Laurence Anholt

TED SMART

There was once a little girl who didn't like books. Her mum liked books. Her dad liked books. Her brother, Jack, *loved* books and he couldn't even read.

"Books are boring," the little girl said.
And she stamped out into the garden to find
a real adventure.

"Keep an eye on Jack!" called the little
girl's mother as Jack sat down with his book
on the grass.

The little girl searched for something
exciting in the garden. She didn't find much.
When she turned round, Jack wasn't looking
at his book...

...he was crawling *inside* it!
"Come back, Jack!" called the little girl.

But Jack was already gone.
She crawled in after him.

Inside the book was a steep green hill and at the bottom someone was crying.

"Oh no, he's hurt himself!" said the little girl.

But it wasn't Jack crying at the bottom of the hill. It was Jill.

"Jack fell down – and now he's run off," Jill said.

"Oh dear!" said the little girl. "Come back, Jack!"

The little girl hadn't gone far when she saw a strange crowd standing outside a house.

"This is the house that Jack built," said a cow with a crumpled horn.

"Jack isn't old enough to build houses," said the little girl. "He can't even read yet."

"But he's a clever lad," said the cow. "Nimble and quick, too. Just watch him jump over that candlestick!"

"Oh dear," said the little girl...

"COME BACK, JACK!"

The little girl found herself up in the clouds.
She couldn't see Jack. What she could see was
a huge castle with its great door wide open.

The little girl crept through the castle
door – and there was Jack, sitting in a corner,
eating a Christmas pie. She was just about to
tell him to take out his thumb and eat politely,
when the whole castle began to shake.

A great voice roared:

"FEE FI FO FUM,

The little girl took hold of Jack's hand and they ran out of the castle as quickly as they could. But the giant had seen them.

"FUM FO FEE FI,

I WANT THOSE CHILDREN IN A PIE!"

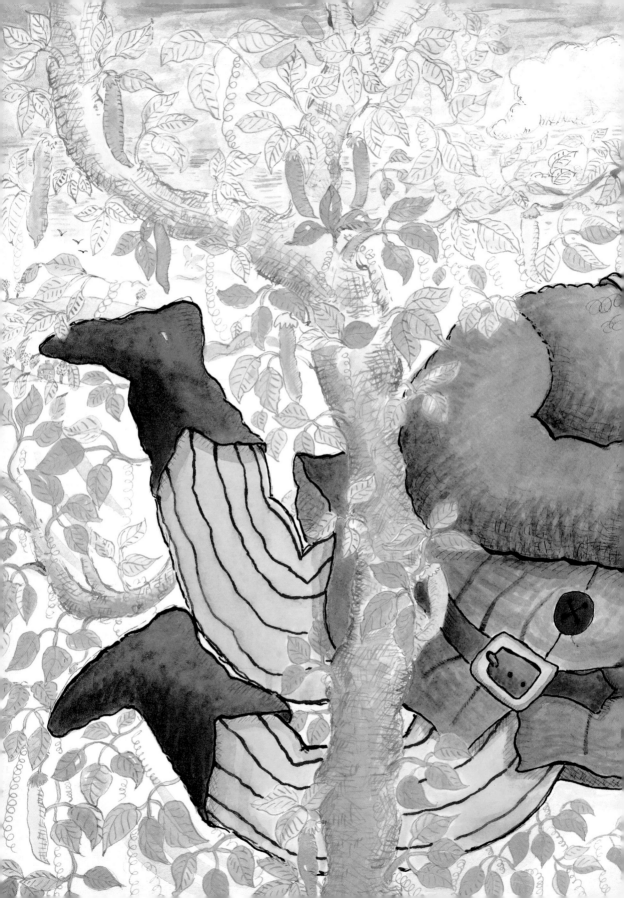

Just in time, they found a beanstalk growing
up through the clouds. They started to climb
down it, but the giant was getting closer.
He was about to grab them when...

…they reached the end of the book and tumbled out into their very own garden.

The giant's huge hairy hand stretched out after them, but Jack banged the book shut.

From inside the book came a faraway roar:

"FEE FI FO FUM, NOW I'VE GONE AND HURT MY THUMB!"

"Well," said the little girl, "perhaps books aren't boring after all!"

Then she and Jack lay on the grass, and they laughed and laughed and laughed.

Jack and the Beanstalk

Jack be Nimble

Jack be nimble,
Jack be quick,
Jack jump over
The candlestick.

Jack and Jill

Jack and Jill went up the hill
To fetch a pail of water;
Jack fell down and broke his crown,
And Jill came tumbling after.

The House that Jack Built

This is the farmer sowing his corn
that kept the cock that crowed in the morn
that waked the priest all shaven and shorn
that married the man all tattered and torn
that kissed the maiden all forlorn
that milked the cow with the crumpled horn
that tossed the dog that worried the cat
that killed the rat that ate the malt
that lay in the house that Jack built.

Little Jack Horner

Little Jack Horner
Sat in the corner,
Eating a Christmas pie;
He put in his thumb,
And pulled out a plum,
And said, What a good boy am I!